For Nicola, Eliza, Jack and Tom
~ A M

For Miles, with love
~ J M

LITTLE TIGER PRESS
1 The Coda Centre, 189 Munster Road,
London SW6 6AW
www.littletigerpress.com

First published in Great Britain 1995
This edition published 2006

A CIP catalogue record for this book is
available from the British Library

Little Teddy Left Behind

Anne Mangan

Joanne Moss

LITTLE TIGER PRESS
London

Little Teddy woke up and sneezed loudly. Nobody
heard him because no one was there. Nicola and Jack
had moved to a new house.

"I'm all alone," said Teddy. "They've left me behind.
They never were very good at packing. I'm all dusty too,"
he said, and he sneezed and he sneezed.

It grew dark, and at last Teddy went to sleep again . . .

. . . until the next morning when
the cleaning lady's dog spotted him
and picked him up.

"What have you there?" asked the
lady, and when she saw how grubby
Teddy was, she grabbed him with
her big hands . . .

. . . and popped him into the
washing machine!

"Oh help!" cried Little Teddy,
but nobody heard his tiny squeak.

It was dreadful in the washing
machine. Teddy was whirled
round and round until he was
quite dizzy. He growled his very
loudest growl, but nobody came
to rescue him.

At last he was
spun dry and the
machine stopped.
Teddy lay there
among all the
damp clothes,
wondering what
would happen next.

The cleaning lady opened the machine door and took out Teddy. "You're not quite dry yet," she said.

"I am so!" growled Little Teddy, but she took no notice and pinned him upside-down on a clothesline.

"I'd rather be dirty and the right way up!" he cried, but of course nobody heard his tiny squeak.

It was windy and
Teddy swung back
and forth on the clothesline.
It was exciting in a way, like flying in space.
    All at once the line broke, and Teddy fell down, down,
down into the grass. Butterflies flew all around him and
bees buzzed over his head. Teddy liked the bright cheerful
butterflies, but he was a bit afraid of the bees.
    "You scare me," he squeaked, but the bees were too
busy to hear him.
    Suddenly Teddy felt hot breath in his ear.

"Oh no!" he cried. "It's that dog again!"

The dog seized the little bear in his big teeth and pushed through a very prickly hedge into the next garden.

"Oh, my poor fur!" gasped Teddy.

A lady looked up as the dog rushed on to her lawn. "Ugh, he's got a rat in his mouth!" she screamed and threw a gardening glove at them.

"I'm not a rat!" growled Teddy.

The dog ran out through
the garden gate into a wood.
"Oh, I do wish he'd drop me," thought Teddy
and at last he did. The dog spotted a rabbit and ran off,
leaving Teddy behind.

Teddy lay very still, hoping the dog wouldn't come back.
It was quiet in the wood – but not for long. Two children
came rushing towards him.

"Hey, a little teddy!" cried one of the children.

"That's me," thought Teddy. "Now what?"

He soon found out.

"Catch!" the boy yelled and poor Teddy
was tossed from one to the other until he felt quite
sick. Jack and Nicola had never played with him like this.

At last the children grew tired of their game and the
girl flung Little Teddy high into the air.

Up, up, up he sailed, right into the branches of a tall
tree. No sooner had he landed than he heard an angry
chittering noise.

"Trying to steal my nuts, are you?"

Teddy looked down. At the end of his branch a squirrel was glaring at him. Teddy tried to explain about the boy and girl and their awful game of catch, but the squirrel didn't seem to hear. "This is my tree!" he said, giving Teddy a sudden push. The little bear fell down, down, down . . .

. . . and landed on a wooden floor.

He was lying there, getting his breath back and worrying whether Jack and Nicola would ever find him again, when he heard children's voices. He tried his growl and he tried his squeak, but they were too small for the children to hear him.

The floor was as dusty as the empty room he had left behind. Once again Little Teddy began to sneeze and sneeze. The sneezes were louder than the growl and the squeak, and at last the voices came nearer . . .

"Look, there's a ladder!"

"It's a tree house!"

Two faces were peering at him – two faces he knew very well!

"It's Little Teddy!" cried Jack. "How did he get into our new garden? I thought he was all packed up."

"I don't know, but it doesn't matter," said Nicola, giving Teddy a hug. "We've found Teddy *and* a tree house."

"It's Teddy's tree house," said Jack. "He found it."

His very own house! Little Teddy liked the idea.

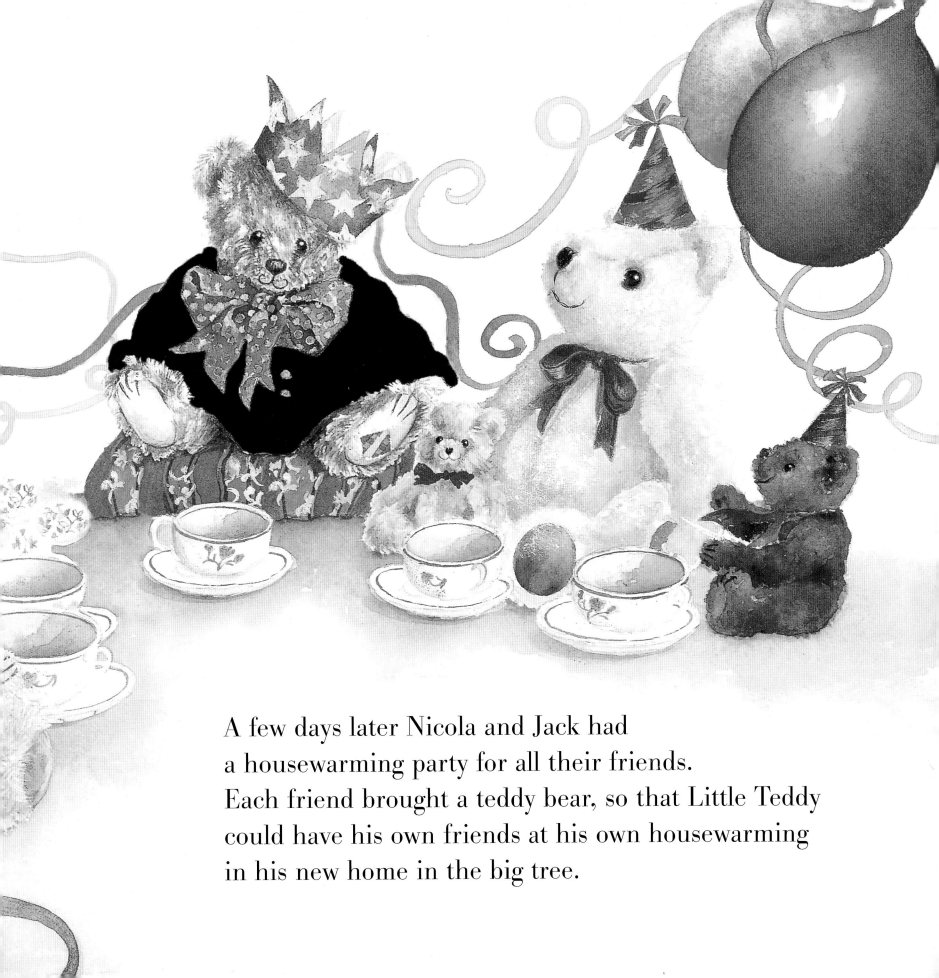

A few days later Nicola and Jack had
a housewarming party for all their friends.
Each friend brought a teddy bear, so that Little Teddy
could have his own friends at his own housewarming
in his new home in the big tree.